"Enjoyable and interesting. I found Millers' knowledge of Tibet and Buddhism fascinating. He writes a fine story, in what is quite obviously a labor of love. A must book to obtain."

—Gary Lovisi in *SHERLOCK HOLMES:*
The Great Detective in Paperback

"The solving of the crime by Holmes-Sigerson was true Canon indeed. A pleasure."

—John Bennett Shaw, Sherlock Holmes authority

THOMAS KENT MILLER'S
Holmes Behind the Veil Series

Book 1
SHERLOCK HOLMES
ON THE ROOF OF THE WORLD;
Or, The Adventure of the Wayfaring God

Book 2
THE GREAT DETECTIVE
AT THE CRUCIBLE OF LIFE;
Or, The Adventure of the Rose of Fire

Book 3
THE SUSSEX BEEKEEPER
AT THE DAWN OF TIME
Or, The Adventure of the Star of Wonder

Holmes Behind The Veil, Book 1

SHERLOCK HOLMES

ON THE ROOF OF THE WORLD;

Or, The Adventure of the Wayfaring God

From the Journal of

Leo Vincey, Esq.

Being a Further Chronicle of the Exploits of Horace Holly

and Leo Vincey, as Previously Published in the Volumes

"She" and "Ayesha: The Return of She"

By L. Horace Holly

Edited and with a Foreword and Notes by

Thomas Kent Miller

Paperback ISBN 978-1-78705-144-7
ePub ISBN 978-1-78705-145-4
PDF ISBN 978-1-78705-146-1

Published in the UK by MX Publishing
335 Princess Park Manor, Royal Drive,
London, N11 3GX
www.mxpublishing.co.uk

Cover design by Brian Belanger

Potala Palace illustration by Linda Villareal

For Nicholas Lawrence Miller

The guiding star of our existence.

CONTENTS

Foreword   1

Introduction   11

I   Sigerson the Norwegian   16

II   The Fate of Poor Paljori   32

III   The Dalai Lama Beckons   41

IV   The Dalai Lama's Story   51

V   The Monk of Long Ago   55

VI   An Undertaker and a Doctor   62

VII   Sigerson's Solutions   65

The Gospel of Issa   76

Conclusion   87

Addendum   99

Foreword

As I prepare Leo Vincey's manuscript for publication, there is one thing, I find, that especially saddens me: namely that, in this entire heretofore unknown Sherlock Holmes adventure, there is only one oblique reference to Watson—Dr. John H. Watson, friend, confidant, and biographer of the great detective. What, I ask myself, is a Holmes story without his trusty Watson?

As is known, nearly all the lost adventures that have come to light since the passing of the principal characters have been through an agency connected somehow either to Watson or his estate, or to Holmes's estate. But even that cannot be said for the tale you are about to read. It is apparent, I think, that Watson never had any knowledge of either the manuscript or the incident which it describes, and that Holmes kept the matter entirely to himself, as he was in the habit of doing with so many particulars of his life.

Be that as it may, I will now explain how the manuscript came to the attention of this editor. My wife and I lived in a secluded part of a rustic town midway between San Francisco and Silicon Valley. In April of 1984, our neighbor up the court from us, Jan Needleman, was preparing to travel to Nepal. As an employee of an airline, Jan could travel virtually anywhere without cost. The day before she was to take off via British Airways to Calcutta, she called us and asked if we would keep an eye on her house for three weeks and bring in her mail. At the time, we were still fairly new to the neighborhood; I barely knew Jan and had no idea that she was about to embark on such a grand adventure.

As it happened, as I spoke to her over the phone in my basement office, I was surrounded by stacks of books about the Himalayan region—*Seven Years in Tibet* and *Return to Tibet* by Heinrich Harrer, *The Secret Exploration of Tibet* by Peter Hopkick, *The Third Eye* by T. Lobsang Rampa, *The Trekker's Guide to the Himalaya* by Hugh Swift, *The Way to Shambhala* by Edwin Bernbaum, and *The Arun: A Natural History of the World's Deepest Valley* by Edward W. Cronin, Jr., to name a few. As coincidence would have it, during the several months previous, I had developed an interest in that part of Central Asia called the Roof of the World and had done extensive research on the subject with the intention of parlaying the information into some sort of book. The fact is that Himalayan trekking had become a popular pastime among young urban professionals, and interest in the region had simply picked up appreciably. It seemed to me inevitable that a new travel book of some sort or a reference book about northern India, Nepal, Tibet, and the Himalayas was virtually guaranteed to succeed.

Such was my background in the subject when, out of the blue, Jan called to say she was leaving the next day. Naturally I was very excited for her and was about to summarize all of the above for her and to ask her to be alert on my behalf for anything of interest of an anecdotal nature that I could use in my book. But before I could broach the subject, my wife drove in from the market beeping the car horn, indicating that she needed help unloading the car. Knowing where my duty lay, I simply wished Jan fun on her trip and agreed to look after things for her while she was gone.

Life went on as usual, and at the end of the third week Jan returned—at once enchanted by her experience and disappointed. Don't ask me how she did it, but despite all her research into the trip, two critical facts had evaded her: April may be the best time of the year to witness the miracle of Nepal's rhododendrons, but it is also the month that the entire Himalayan range is socked in by mist and fog so that not even the slightest pinnacle is visible.

She enjoyed herself nonetheless, especially her excursions in the towns and cities on her trip, and she returned with a small gift for us for our trouble: a packet of handcrafted stationery.

The stationery was in a lovely ten-inch-by-seven-and-one-half-inch envelope covered with a blue and red stencil of what appeared to be a conch shell repeated innumerable times so that very little of the beige paper showed through. The flap on the envelope was secured by a strand of red string tied in a bow knot. As I handled this token of appreciation from the other side of the planet, I was immediately impressed with the craft involved and the brilliant colors. I undid the string tie and pulled out the contents—several sheets of red-stenciled "Dambar Kumari" paper with black-stenciled matching envelopes. An enclosed rough explanatory note indicated that the paper was named after "a famous beauty in the Nepalese court" who had been the first to wear printed cloth, and explained that "two hundred years ago in the Himalayan Kingdom of Nepal a group of men started the tradition of textile printing," having learned the technique from the Muslims of northern India.

As I riffled through the stationery, I saw that there were several consecutive sheets in the back that had already

4

been written on. These sheets proved to be much older than the others, of a different paper altogether, and brittle besides. The writing was in English and in an elaborate hand. Questioning Jan, she had no idea how these sheets got into the stationery packet. She had purchased this gift, as well as a number of other souvenirs, trinkets for friends and family, and the like, from various street vendors and market bazaars on her travels. One can only guess how the sheets got into the hands of a Nepalese peasant, or of what went on in his or her mind: probably some notion of economizing or something of the sort. It was impossible to say.

What follows is the contents of those sheets in toto, edited only to improve the title from the original "Journal of Events in Lhasa" to one of a more Watsonian cast, to add a few applicable epigraphs, to correct or update spelling (e.g., "Tibet" for "Thibet"), and to add appropriate chapter titles and notes.

Whether the manuscript is authentic and whether the events it chronicles really happened is anyone's guess. Whether what it records has any basis at all in reality or is just the rambling writings of a delirious man also is anyone's guess. For my part, I believe that the manuscript is authentic, was penned by one Leo Vincey in 1891, that the events chronicled did in fact happen as described, and that it was left in the safekeeping of Sherlock Holmes himself. How it passed from Holmes's hands into a packet of stationery ninety-three years later is a tale that may never be told. We may simply be pleased that it did reach our world intact so that its contents can be shared with our generation.

But one fantasy persists. What if Holmes had in fact delivered the manuscript into the hands of his friend, Dr. Watson, as he had no doubt intended? How would the good doctor have edited it? What would have been his approach? What sort of droll commentary or imaginative framing device would he have included to temper the impact of the story, as he was wont to do with the more sensitive of his friend's exploits? Perhaps such questions are pointless, but they are seductive.

Two points, it seems to me, are clear. This is one of the few stories to come to light regarding events involving "Sigerson," the fictitious name Holmes went by during the nearly three years of his Great Hiatus (a point that he discusses in "The Adventure of the Empty House," and which is elaborated on at great length in Baring-Gould's biography of the sleuth and also in his *Annotated Sherlock Holmes*). Besides this extraordinary claim to fame, the following tale also has the distinction of being the true first sequel to Horace Holly's famous journal, *She*, which was published in 1887 under the byline of Holly's agent, Henry Rider Haggard. The only heretofore known sequel, *Ayesha: The Return of She*, was published in 1904 and records events that occurred some twenty years after *She*. This new tale is a record of events that occurred *between* the previously published adventures.

For those unfamiliar with the events that precede this new story, I have included the following synopsis of She and the pertinent early sections of Ayesha.

The adventures of Horace Holly and Leo Vincey, in brief, as recorded in She *plus some early incidents from* Ayesha:

Late at night, Ludwig Horace Holly, a student at Cambridge University, is studying in his rooms when his friend, Vincey, unexpectedly arrives with a heavy strong-box. Vincey explains that he is dying, and asks Holly to act as guardian to his son, Leo. Vincey does in fact die, and the years roll quickly by. When Leo turns twenty-five, he opens the box his father had left him. In it he finds a broken potsherd inscribed with ancient writings.

The inscriptions tell a weird story: Leo's ancestor Kallikrates, a priest of Isis, had broken faith and fled Egypt with a young princess, Amenartas. The inscriptions also tell of the queen of a savage people—a white goddess—and a strange Pillar of Fire, which she had shown Kallikrates and Amenartas. The queen fell in love with Kallikrates and, in a fit of jealousy, slew him, but Amenartas escaped to give birth to Kallikrates's son. The writing ends in Amenartas' plea that the son she was leaving behind, or another courageous descendant, avenge her against the Queen of the Pillar of Fire.

Leo and Horace take up the quest and after many trials come to the hidden African city of Kôr, carved out of solid rock, where reigns the mysterious Ayesha, She-Who-Must-Be-Obeyed. Ayesha explains to Horace that she has been living in her hidden city for two thousand years without news of the outside world. Time means nothing to her; nor can death touch her.

The next day, Ayesha visits Leo, who is dying of fever from a wound. When she enters his room and sees him for the first time, she draws back in astonishment. Leo has the features of the dead Kallikrates: He is the man she has loved and whose rebirth she has awaited for two thousand years. Ayesha then restores Leo's health.

Eventually she persuades Leo and Horace to see the Pillar of Fire for themselves. Leo, though, hesitates to enter the flame as it shoots up from the bowels of the earth. To assuage his fears, Ayesha enters the fire where she bathed only once before two thousand years earlier. Her features begin to shrivel, her arms grow scrawny and wilt, and before the stunned audience, she shrinks into a small bundle of skin and bones. Why? How? No one knows. Perhaps the flame's magic can only be used once in a lifetime. Three weeks after they penetrated the African interior, the two men emerge and make their way to England.

During a period of morbid isolation in England, Leo and Holly strive to wring some meaning from the joke called Life. Leo's despair is so great, he contemplates suicide. However, a Universal Power greater than his intervenes, providing two separate but related signs—one a dream, the other the sun bursting through a particular cloud formation— that give our adventurers hope once again. At once they arrange to leave for Central Asia. They travel through the snows and mountains of that region for a number of years seeking the solidly real manifestation of the symbols they saw in the signs . . . and seeking the meaning of Ayesha's last words: "I shall come again." For a while they tarry in Lhasa.

T. K. M.

"I traveled for two years in Tibet . . . and amused myself by visiting Lhasa, and spending some days with the head Lama."
—Sherlock Holmes in "The Adventure of the Empty House"

"We are . . . going away again, this time to Central Asia, where, if anywhere upon this Earth, wisdom is to be found . . .
—L. HORACE HOLLY in *She*

The Potala—that most spectacular of Asian palaces—in Lhasa, Tibet.

Introduction

It is Horace who is the incurable chronicler, not I. I'm afraid the arts of writing have never been to my taste, except in regard to the mundane affairs of life. Pen and paper have more often been foreign to me than not despite my university days, but those days are long past and seem remote beyond ken, at least in the light of the events of subsequent years. Indeed, I am writing this account now for two reasons only: The first is that Horace is incapacitated with an ailing heart, or so he believes it is, for we must make do here without Western medicine of any sort. Also, the resident medical authority, who is more a priest than a doctor, concurs with Horace, but, in any event, my friend and foster father is hardly well. Frankly, I believe that his Christian soul has suffered a severe shock of the most profound sort. I can say this with some certainty because I suffer as well, even as I write.

Which brings me to the second purpose for this account. That which Holly and I and a Norwegian chap named Sigerson learned or deduced in recent weeks is of such incalculable import that a record of the whole affair must be made, for better or for worse. Of course, there is the temptation to simply disregard the evidence and to "let sleeping dogs lie" as they say; yet I cannot in conscience simply abandon a point of knowledge of civilization-shaking import. I suppose that this is the university training coming out in me, or perhaps it is simply a respect for knowledge and truth that I never dreamed I possessed before now. On the other hand, the very prodigious and threatening nature of our discovery could well shake civilization in fact and not at all figuratively. Do I want, I must ask myself, to be accountable for the maelstrom of confusion that must inevitably follow the release of a manuscript such as I am about to set down?

***

So, there are the two poles of the problem with which I am confronted. If only Horace was strong enough now to guide me in this matter as he has guided me in so many matters over the years. Yet I dare not impose on him any part of this quandary, at least at this time, for fear of aggravating his condition. In any case, I have made my decision: While they are still fresh in my mind, the circumstances must be set down as well as I understand them. At the least, this is my duty as an intelligent man.

Yet, neither do I rate lightly my current circumstances: Where am I? In the vicinity of Lhasa, Tibet, where to my knowledge no other Europeans—and no other Westerners—other than Horace and Sigerson have been allowed to sojourn during this century. What am I doing here? Even more importantly, when do I intend to return to England or, for that matter, to any part of the world that is considered "civilized," "a safe harbor," "a port in a storm," et cetera? The answer to that is of course when I find Ayesha, which may be next week or in a thousand years. Knowing these facts, then, an ordinary man would be naturally prone to ask further: If even the manuscript were to be written, what is the probability that it would even reach a discerning world? What chance will such a fragile thing as a manuscript—written on old notebooks—ever have of reaching the world beyond these encircling mountains? So it is that I've determined to do what I must, and then let the dice fall where they may. I cannot say for certain whether or not God intercedes in human affairs, yet I believe He must, at least in matters of consequence, as this affair must be considered.

I will write, the dice will roll, and the rest is in Hands far greater than mine.

Five or six years ago, following our return to England from Kôr, Horace busied himself recounting in some detail the adventures we experienced both approaching and in that fabulous land, which we were the first white men to enter in two thousand years, or so Ayesha led us to believe. And though this woman, who is so much more than a mere woman, may be the veritable sun lighting my path, I have known her on occasion to alter the truth to suit her own needs. Thus, whether this bit of information is totally accurate or not, I know not.*

In any case, after Horace had completed setting down all the strange things that happened to us, we deliberated for some time to decide what to do with his "book," as we were wont to call it at that time. We mutually decided that nothing would happen to it so long as either one of us lived. But since it contained an account of things we believed to be of especial

---

* Editor's note: Allan Quatermain of *King Solomon's Mines* fame, records in *She and Allan* an adventure he had in Kôr in 1872.— T.K.M.

even "unparalleled interest," which was, I believe, the phrase we bandied about all during this time, we would make arrangements with a certain agent for it to be made public following our demises, however and whenever those may occur. Then, in the end, we decided to leave with the agent the final determination. As it turned out, however, circumstances arose quite unexpectedly the result of which was that Horace and I prepared to leave England in some haste. I understand from Sigerson that this agent found the script worthy enough to publish and that it enjoyed some popularity.

I mention these particulars only so that whoever may come into possession of this journal will understand that there is a long preface, already published, which may be of some interest or use insofar as it may put into some kind of perspective the nature of events that brought us to Tibet in the first place.

But I am wandering; I have a tale to tell and all of the preceding is tangential at best, only casting light on how it was we were in the chief library of the capital city of Tibet in the year 1891.

L. V.

CHAPTER ONE

Sigerson the Norwegian

Horace and I were again deep in the archives of the library of Lhasa. We had made up our minds that this would be our last visit to those stone catacombs; but we had little hope of finding what we were looking for. For nearly half a year we had virtually bivouacked in the venerable institution, opening countless books, unrolling some few scrolls, scanning line after line and page after page, seeking some clue as to the whereabouts of, or any reference at all to, the volcanic peak above which towered the symbol of Life of the Egyptians—the crux-ansata,* which Ayesha led me to in a dream. Indeed, it was this dream—and a waking vision that Horace and I shared fast on the heels of the dream—that prompted our sudden leave-taking from England. It had been made quite clear to us—by what powers I cannot say—that Ayesha was keeping her oath to come again, and that we would find her in Central Asia. All we need do is go there and seek her.

---

* Editor's note: More commonly called an Ankh.—T.K.M.

As it turned out, five or six years of seeking have succeeded only in determining where she is not and haven't given us a clue as to the location of the Loop of Life, the visionary symbol of which we are certain was given to us as a sign, rather as an X that marks the spot, the spot being, of course, the true and ennobling love which I must seek to find fulfillment, at least in this life, which, despite Ayesha's tales, is the only life of which I know; and I cannot live without this woman. After all, didn't our Lord say, "Seek and ye shall find; knock and the door will open" or words to that effect? Well, if ever there is an award given for seeking, certainly Horace and I should win the prize.

***

As I was saying, Horace and I were searching for the last time for any possible clue in the books, for none of the lamas or any of the other estimable locals to whom we had spoken had any knowledge or the slightest concept of that which we sought. Fortunately, our backgrounds in language and the long years we have spent trekking about this land and its high terrain have given us sufficient familiarity with the Tibetan language—both spoken and written—so that we were quite able to pick our way through the books and scrolls and such things with confidence. We were, in fact, looking over again some volumes which had seemed promising some months previously, but which had proved barren, at least at that time. Our intent was to take a last look at these works and then depart, that is to say, plunge ahead, or over, the most prodigious mountain country on the planet with the intention of continuing our quest.

We were intent on this business in a corner of an antechamber, which had evidently been hewn from solid rock and which branched off a main corridor, when there came to us the sound of scuffling not unlike rats in a wall (not likely in this rocky place), then a muffled curse in English, more scuffling, then the unmistakably pungent smell of a waxed Vesta being lit, and finally the totally incongruous yet delightfully familiar aroma of smoking shag. Horace and I became aware of the first scuffling at the same moment and we both looked up from our respective volumes and glanced quizzically at one another.

At the sound of the English voice, our eyes opened wide together and I mouthed silently, "What the devil!" Then as the succession of extraordinary little events seemed to reach its conclusion, in a hushed voice I said to Horace, "It's been years since we smelled tobacco like that. Heavens! It's like being in an English drawing room again. Who on earth could be smoking the stuff in this place?"

***

Horace's reaction was to place his finger along his nose, indicating quiet. Frankly I was irritated by this gesture. This seemed to me to be a time for exclamations and such, not the nervous concealment of a scared rabbit. I was about to say as much, when there came a clear voice across the stacks calling out in English.

"Hallo! I say, is anyone here? That is, are there Europeans here? There are, after all, quite a few Tibetans about." Following this, there came a chuckle.

Horace put his hand on my arm as I was about to impulsively reply. For a while there was silence, then the voice came again.

"Well, of course, I can understand your timidity. We are a long way from home, aren't we . . . ? Yet, I can't help but feel somewhat put off. Frankly, I long for a Western face."

Well, even Horace's customary caution melted under such sentiments, and we both called out.

"Hallo. Stay still. We'll come to you."

It must be understood that it was hardly a matter of simply stepping over to the source of the voice. The library was, or is, a virtual maze, and one moved from one place to another only by trial and error. Over the months, Horace and I had learned our way about the place, but still it was not wise to go rushing off in some direction without taking one's bearings, noting landmarks, so to speak, and so forth.

"Most certainly, my dear fellows," came the voice. "I wouldn't dream of moving. I'll just chatter on till we meet. My, my, it certainly is unexpected to discover in a remote place like this, if not one's countrymen, at least Westerners with whom a man can share a smoke and perhaps some gossip of matters of mutual interest." He kept talking like this for a couple of minutes as Horace and I picked our way through the dusty stacks of long board-covered books. Then, "Hallo, there, you're getting warm . . . around the next bend then . . . and there you are!"

There standing languidly before us, his back against a shelf, was a tall man, somewhat over six feet, with piercing eyes that had a bit of humor about them. Beneath these eyes was a straight, sharp nose and then a full growth of dark beard, much as both Horace and I possess. (Shaving is a civilized custom that one soon learns to do without in a remote and bitter land such as Tibet.)

"My name is Sigerson," the fellow said, and he put down the book he was holding and held out his hand. "I'm a Norwegian up to no good, I'm afraid."

Horace and I shook the man's hand, Horace saying, "But your English is so good." But before either Horace or I had a chance to introduce ourselves, Sigerson went on.

"Oh, that is easy, you know. Much of my adult life has been spent in England. I'm rather a free spirit, flitting between the two countries and points between and beyond as—" he indicated the space around him "—you can see readily enough. But I must know, how did you find the workmanship of the gold work at the market this afternoon? It is most satisfying to know there is, after all, some craftsmanship and pride and such things left in the world, even in this day and age, though one must look for it in Tibet!"

Horace and I gave one another a questioning glance, then Horace looked up at the man, fixing him hard in the eye.

"Now, see here, sir! If you saw us there, why didn't you come forward? It seems to me the only proper thing to do, after all."

Sigerson smiled impishly. "But, my good man, I did not see you there today. In fact, it's been days since I've been to the market. No, no. I saw clearly that the two of you had been at the goldsmith's today from the minute specks of gold dust I see glinting on your fingertips, from that and from the orange mud staining the edges of your boots. That particular mud is comprised of a soil rich in ocher clay, and in my wanderings to date I've noticed it only in the vicinity of the open-air market. That the stains show signs of still being wet indicates that you were there only this afternoon. Quite simple, actually."

"Impertinence is more like it!" Horace harrumphed. My foster father, as I do, likes matters straightforward and simple. We both understand "simple," and Sigerson's idea of "simple" was clearly not ours.

"Now, now, old chap, there is no need to take offense. It's a bit of a hobby of mine to make deductions from the obvious things that few others heed. For instance, it is apparent that having achieved your ends at the goldsmith's shop, you strolled up to Palkhor Street for a nourishing repast of yak cheese and buttered tea."

At this point, I was aghast. Horace, I could see, was quite as dumbfounded. He inhaled and exhaled a deep breath. "'Impertinence' I said, and 'impertinence' I meant, dash it all! What right do you have snooping on us, following us about as though we were a couple of criminals! A fine how-do-you-do this is!" Horace's voice was quite naturally raising. It was my turn to put a restraining hand on his arm. After all, we had only just met the man, and it was certainly too soon to get into a brawl.

"Perhaps, Horace, Mr. Sigerson would be kind enough to explain."

"Certainly. I must learn either to keep my little revelations to myself or to broach them in a more subtle fashion. Actually, I can't blame you for your agitation. There are those who say I am somewhat smug, but I honestly can't help myself. It seems to be a part of my natural condition. In any case, responding to your query, in your beards are numerous morsels of yak cheese which indicates what your last meal must have been, and the mule dung covering in spots the previously cited mud on your boots is evidence that from the market you traveled, by what route I'm not entirely clear, to east Lhasa where the mule traffic is centralized by ordinance, and I happen to know of a fine little cheese shop in the vicinity, which happens to be on Palkhor Street."

"And the buttered tea?" I asked.

"My good man, who in this country doesn't drink vast amounts of the stuff at every available opportunity?"

"A point well taken. Horace, I believe we both owe Mr. Sigerson an apology. He certainly seems on the up and up."

Horace colored and held out his hand. "I suppose so. But this sort of legerdemain or mental prestidigitation or whatever you may call it will get you in trouble some day, Sigerson, mark my words, unless you learn to curb yourself. But I'm afraid Leo and myself have been in error ourselves by not introducing ourselves. I am—"

"No, no. Let me guess. You are the indomitable Ludwig Horace Holly and this is Leo Vincey."

"Why man," I said, grasping the man's hand again, "did you read that from the mud and dung?"

"Not at all. Leo Vincey and Horace Holly hot on the trail of She-Who-Must-Be-Obeyed, no doubt."

There was no end to the shocks that this Sigerson presented. As a man, Horace and I stepped back in surprise, our jaws dropping. Though we may have at times asked directions to certain geological or architectural landmarks which we had reason to believe marked our goal, never during our travels in Asia had we mentioned what that ultimate goal was.

"Gentlemen, don't be so surprised," Sigerson interjected. "In this year 1891, I would venture to guess that half of Europe and much of America besides know exactly who you are and have reveled and despaired vicariously with you on your adventure into Central Africa."

Then I understood. "So the man to whom Horace sent his account of those days has seen that it was published."

"Yes, and to worldwide acclaim."

"My word," Horace said.

"And, I'm sure, insomuch as your agent is by all indications a man of honor, I would think that he has set aside some percentage of the royalties for the event of your return. Quite a few quid, I would venture."

Horace was about to interject, when Sigerson continued, "No, no, my good man, I know what you are about to say: that you had specified to the man that he could do with the manuscript as he pleased and that he could keep whatever monies might be derived from that decision. True enough, for that is also common knowledge, yet as I said, I feel certain your agent, who has surely become a rich man acting on your behalf, has made arrangements so that the author of the book can enjoy some of those fruits as well."

I chose this moment to speak my thoughts. "Mr. Sigerson, this is news indeed, though I must say it is a bit disconcerting to know that half the world is privy to one's most intimate desires." Here I looked at Horace. "Horace, when I agreed to let you send your manuscript to that agent, I never thought that our quest would be held up to public inspection to be talked of and bantered about as though we were the subjects of some tasteless governmental scandal."

"Nor I, Leo. I am decimated to hear this."

"My man!" exclaimed Sigerson. "I am telling you that you are a wealthy man now. You need only to return to Europe to claim your own."

"Ah, but there are catches here," Horace said. "I am, and I'm sure I can speak for Leo as well—("Here, here!" I said)—quite content being where I am doing what I'm doing. Neither the money nor the suggestion to return home interest me one jot."

"Please," Sigerson said, "I did not intend to upset either of you. These matters of which I spoke are, as I said, common knowledge to all except the principals involved, and I ought to have been more sensitive than to have callously brandished this knowledge at your expense. I ask your forgiveness. But, also, I must ask, how fruitful has the sequel been?"

"Fruitless," I answered, hardly able to stifle a groan, whereupon I described the nature of the dream that sent us to Asia and how to this date we had succeeded not one whit.

"We had hoped to find here in Lhasa some clue to the location of the looped pillar. We have been here for six months to no avail. It was our intention to set out tomorrow to the northeast. These last six years have been utterly futile except to chalk off a bit of territory."

"Excuse me, gentlemen, but I can't help but wonder that, despite the nature of your previous adventures, you would spend your lives tramping about the Tibetan wilderness on the strength of a dream."

"But, sir, there was more!" I ejaculated. "Following my dream, there occurred a most spectacular display in the heavens that affirmed the dream without question. It was the moment of dawn and the English sky was clouded over. But as we looked, the clouds broke apart and formed the definite shape of a Loop of Life at the rim of a fiery crater, the fire being the sun breaking between the clouds, and as it broke a sharp ray of crimson light shot through the hole in the loop. I assure you the phenomenon was quite spectacular, though in a moment it was gone. It is on the combined strength of the dream and the vision—which obviously was more than a vision since it entailed somehow rearranging the fabric of the very heavens—that we have based our quest, and it is this memory which girds us daily."

"Indeed," Sigerson said, "it seems odd that a mere coincidence would provide the impetus for a quest that has already lasted five or six years and Lord knows how much longer, not to mention the privations and tribulations."

"My good man," I said, "you cannot know the power that that 'mere coincidence' had, nor the influence it had on our very souls. Believe me, sir, that was no mere coincidence . . . no, not by any means. If anything, I for one consider it the very Grace of God."

"But sir," Horace said after a pause in our conversation, "you have the advantage knowing all there is to know about us, but we know nothing of you."

"Oh, that is easily rectified. I'm a world traveler, a bit of a naturalist, and have received a special commission from the combined crowns of Scandinavia to explore the nature of the Yeti, or the so-called Abominable Snowman, as the press back home is wont to call the beast. Perchance . . . have you had experiences or heard tales in your travels that I might catalogue?"

"No, sir, we have not," answered Horace.

"Pity."

At this moment, we were interrupted by the sudden appearance of the lama whose responsibility it was to oversee the library. He was grimacing and seemed quite shaken.

"Gentlemen," he said in his native Tibetan, "I smell smoke. No, no. That is not allowed. No smoking in the library. This is strictly forbidden. Please leave; it is time to go now. Go, go." Sigerson held up the pipe, which he had been sucking all through our conversation, and used it to gesture to the nearest of the many yak-butter lamps sputtering and smoking along the walls, and which Tibetans universally use to brighten the dark.

"I don't understand," he said in fluent Tibetan, "How could a little smoke from my pipe be of concern when the entire library is lit by flaming lamps under far less control than—"

At this point, the lama interrupted Sigerson with a great sweep of his yellow robes.

"Blasphemy! Oh, we will rue the day we ever allowed white men into our midst. But that is not the point. I am head lama of this library and I say that you must go. Now go! Do not ask questions. Go! Do not interrupt. Go!"

Sigerson looked plaintively at his pipe, which had now gone out. "I'm terribly sorry," he said. "This is my error entirely. I was so involved in my research that the pipe came out by reflex. Be assured it will not happen again." He stirred the shag ash* in his pipe with the untreated end of a Vesta, knocked the pipe empty against his boot heel, and pocketed the offensive instrument.

"Without delay," the lama, whose name was Brother Paljori, said emphatically. He waved us on as though we were so many goats. "Out, out, out! Now, be gone! The Library of Lhasa is closed to you. Begone!"

It was at this point that I lost control. "Now see here, Brother Paljori, what is the meaning of this? My foster father and I have been studying peacefully amongst your stacks for almost six months. We have done nothing wrong. Why are you being so rude over an oversight made by our friend here? Besides that, we intend to leave Lhasa tomorrow, as you well know for we have spoken of it often these last days. I don't understand why you have chosen this moment to be immensely rude and to upbraid us about a matter so small as smoking a pipe."

Horace put a cautionary hand on my arm. I shook it off and glowered at the lama who held his ground, neither elaborating nor explaining our offense or his desires any more than he had already done. Well, the upshot of the matter was that we consented to leave and Paljori shepherded us out. As we exited, and just before the vast bronze doors closed behind us, we saw Paljori bow to us, from force of habit I suppose, since he wasn't particularly enamoured of us at that moment.

CHAPTER TWO

The Fate of Poor Paljori

"Most peculiar," I said as we made our way down the long staircase, "I wonder what got into him."

"I believe the man was more agitated than he let on," Sigerson said. "His distress over my smoking was largely a ruse, and was symptomatic of a more troubled underlying condition. Of that I am certain."

"Whatever the case," Horace said, "if that's his attitude, I'll be glad when we leave tomorrow."

We continued to discuss Paljori's peculiar behavior, not making any headway, but, caught up in conversation, strode off to that very same cheese shop that Sigerson had named when observing our boots. We found a rough table, ordered the simple fare available there, and began to exchange news and experiences. It was heartening to hear from Sigerson that Gladstone had come to power soon after we left England, for I am frankly all for Irish home rule, but I was disheartened that he lost out to Salisbury shortly thereafter. Certainly Salisbury is a fine man, but I always felt he was a bit of a pawn, working for the great commercial interests.

Sigerson says the man has been much involved in the partitioning of Africa, at least to the time Sigerson left Europe. It seems, also, that Queen Victoria's jubilee was a gala event, not to be missed by any except by the likes of us. And so Sigerson brought Horace and me up to date concerning our native England and other matters of interest to the Western world of which we were abysmally ignorant due to our long absence, and, for our part, we gave Sigerson our views of our ports of call in Central Asia.

Sigerson seemed just as pleased to meet us as we did to meet him, and eventually we went off to his tiny apartment in the Doring district where he smoked prodigiously and we talked and drank buttered tea into the wee hours.

Sigerson's room was, as ours was, palatial compared to the transient accommodations provided for pilgrims and such, which were generally loathsome at best, small, rancid-smelling, cramped mud affairs with only a ragged scrap of cloth for a door, sleeping half a dozen or more at a time on whatever rough mats they themselves provided. We three, at least, were provided by the head lamas on our respective arrivals with clean rooms. Horace and I shared one at some distance from Sigerson's, equipped with sufficient cots and bedding. I noticed the other accouterments, or what passed as such, in Sigerson's room were similar to those in Horace's and my room: a rude wooden bench, a simple wooden shelf attached at chest level to the wall with nails, a butter lamp, and a real door comprised of two vertical planks held together by two traverse planks.

As for Sigerson's personal effects, there was little enough: a bag under his cot, a second pipe and a row of books on the shelf, and various bits of apparel scattered about. We spoke of many things that night, but mainly of the power of love, of Ayesha, and of a woman in Sigerson's past named Irene.

It was just before dawn, when they say that the hour is the darkest and when we three began to show signs of exhaustion, that we first heard the faint sounds of men yelling and general far-off pandemonium. Of course we were concerned and curious, but not for a moment did we suspect that we would soon be the central characters in a drama of genuinely earth-shattering dimensions.

***

The sounds of running and men crying out came closer. Suddenly Sigerson's door burst open and an army of yellow-and-maroon-clad police monks fell upon us, man-handling us in an uncouth manner, and dragging us out into the street without so much as a word of explanation. My first inclination, of course, was to fight off the wretches, but Horace was able to communicate to me by his expression and a few chosen words that he thought we should stay calm, that there had obviously been a misunderstanding, and that struggling at this time would only lead to further difficulties. Sigerson, at the start of this dismal affair, had struck a stoic expression and merely let himself be dragged. Reflecting that perhaps Horace and Sigerson had reasons for their quiescent attitude, I, too, ceased my struggles and let myself by dragged. (I don't believe we were even given an option to walk.) And dragged we were, through the mud and dung of the street and then east across the Bridge of the Pleiades and on to the Jo-Kang, the Tibetan cathedral.

We were rushed through this temple, the holy of holies of all Buddhist Asia (with an interior to match) then along several corridors and down numerous staircases (I lost track of the turns and switchbacks) and eventually found ourselves in the presence of the High Regent himself. The Dalai Lama was at this time only fourteen-years-old; and since it would be some years before he would be able to govern for himself, the secular aspect of the Tibetan state was run by the Regent, effectively the Dalai Lama's guardian.

He looked little different, to my eye, at least, than the rest of the monks in the room, with shaven head and clad in the traditional brocade robes. It was his bearing that betrayed his high role. He sat behind a plain table, looked at us sharply, and asked us what we meant by killing his librarian.

It can be imagined how we reacted to this query!

"My God, sir, what are you talking about?" were the next words I heard, and they from Horace. "We have hurt no one, let alone killed anyone. Paljori! Are you talking about Paljori? My God, he was fine when we last saw him. Is it he?"

"Of course we are talking of Brother Paljori. His heart was pierced obscenely no more than six hours ago, and a most precious holy relic has been stolen. It is certain that you Europeans are responsible and you must die, but first we must have the book returned to us. Please, if you would be so kind to tell us where you have hidden it, we will then expedite your departure from this incarnation."

"Thank you, your grace." Sigerson now chose to speak up. "It is kind of you to be so considerate of our eternal souls; however, I must disappoint you by enlightening you to the fact that neither my friends here, nor myself, have entertained any violent notions toward any of your kindred, let alone actually hurt anyone, least of all your librarian. Whatever his faults, Paljori certainly didn't deserve to die so horribly. May I ask why it is you believe we are the culprits, since I know that we have been only eating and talking since we last saw Paljori?"

At this point, another lama disengaged himself from the knot of monks standing near the Regent and stated coolly, "Why, it is self-evident! You three are the worst criminals imaginable to accept our hospitality only to murder us at your leisure and steal our most precious belongings."

"At this point," Sigerson said, "I have two questions more: Who, my good man, are you? And what is this precious book of which you speak? Some account of a previous incarnation of the Dalai Lama, no doubt?"

The Regent spread his arm in a grand gesture and said just as grandly, "Why, Mr. Sigerson, this is Wan-Po, Tibet's greatest police monk and solver of crimes. It was he who, ten years ago, solved the mystery of the Dalai Lama's stolen slippers. On his behest, a certain nurse of that time was skinned alive and blinded with burning yak butter. You can believe that no slippers have since disappeared."

I, for one, winced at this terrifying image, but I was determined not to show the least fear. I concentrated on studying our accuser, who bowed and grinned malignly. "Harrumph," snorted Horace, and then in English, "A fine how-do-you-do this is. Falsely accused by a sadistic swine and no recourse at all but trying to talk some sense into the Regent's head. Yet I can't help but think that the cards are stacked against us. Quite a pickle! It appears, Leo, that we will have to fight our way out of this scrape much as we had to fight off the perverts who wanted to burn our heads off with white hot pots.

"Gentlemen," injected Sigerson, "don't give up hope yet. I suspect that the Regent will see the light before long and realize the extent of his mistake."

The Regent made a gesture and the beefy monks who had brought us here tightened their circle around us and were about to lead us Lord knows where, when Sigerson spoke up again:

"My God, man, who do you think you are to accuse us of mischief when you yourself, only minutes ago, were consorting with the Snake Queen, which you know fully well is against all Tibetan law?"

I wish you, dear reader, could have seen the Regent's face at that moment. His mouth fell open and his eyes popped as though he had seen a spectre. In any case, Sigerson seemed successful in catching the man off his guard. Wan-Po first looked at Sigerson and then looked at the Regent and said, "Don't be insane. You are talking to the High Regent himself, sitting in the stead of the Dalai Lama. How dare you talk like that? Absurd! Insane!"

The upshot was that we were dragged off into what was, for all intents and purposes, a dungeon.

"I seemed to have touched a sore point," Sigerson said.

"Bravo, Sigerson!" Horace said. "Here's to having put one over on that bloke. Here! Here!"

"I'm afraid you may have missed the point, Holly," Sigerson replied. "I didn't 'put one over' on that fellow. I simply stated what I knew from evidence readily perceivable to the trained observer."

I saw that Sigerson, despite our situation, was on his high-horse again. Frankly, I was finding his attitude a bit tiresome.

"Well, for goodness sakes, don't leave us dangling," I remarked trying to sound sarcastic. "What did you see that Horace and I were so blind to?"

"Why, it is perfectly straightforward! When we were standing close to the Regent, I smelled an incense that I have reason to believe can only be burnt in the Snake Queen's chambers. Coupled with his disheveled appearance and the rouge on his lips . . . well, there was only one conclusion. But that is neither here nor there. What is important is that Wan-Po will soon be sending for us when he realizes his error."

"But how can you be so certain he will come to that conclusion?" asked Horace.

Sigerson looked at Horace incredulously. "Why, because we didn't murder Paljori, of course!"

CHAPTER THREE

The Dalai Lama Beckons

We bided our time for three days, and, truth to tell, the guards did come for us. But they did not take us directly to Wan-Po. Instead, we were led across the entire city of Lhasa and brought before the fourteen-year-old Dalai Lama himself in his royal quarters in the Potala—that most spectacular of Asian palaces.

I say "brought," but it was hardly this simple. One does not simply step into the Dalai Lama's quarters for a chat. There is a certain protocol or etiquette that must be maintained. The guards were hardly the type to impart this sort of learning to us; monks they may have been, but it seemed to us that some of them were short on the spiritual side of the scale and considerably heavy on the brawn side. So they led us through the unexpectedly drab corridors of that Buddhist Vatican, around and around until we eventually came to a portal, which we passed through, and were brought before a good-natured looking fellow, another monk, of course, for that is the only species of man there, save lamas, who are but high monks, who introduced himself as Brother Sigme.

"Gentlemen," he announced with a flourish, "I am to be your tutor. You are to attend the Presence of the Most High, and I am to instruct you."

Needless to say, we had mixed feelings about this announcement. On one hand, we were flabbergasted that we were to have an unexpected audience with the high lama, but sufficiently angry about our general treatment that none of us reacted in any but a cynical "who on earth do you think you are to be telling us anything?" manner. But, the man was sufficiently pleasant that soon we softened and allowed him to instruct us.

"Enter the room with your eyes down. Walk to a point just five feet from the Dalai Lama. Stick out your tongue, drop to your knees, and bow three times. This is a form of salute. Then kneel with your head bowed and place this silk scarf across His feet. He will then put a scarf across your neck. Finally, slowly rise to your feet and step backwards to the nearest cushion. Now you, Vincey, try it."

I went out of the room, and the lama clapped his hands as a signal for me to enter.

And so it went, with each of us practicing in turn (all the time feeling terribly silly) until several hours went by, though at one point we stopped for a quick lunch of tea and barley. Sigerson and I seemed to get the hang of it fairly quickly, but poor Horace seemed to think the whole business was contemptible and muttered under his breath constantly. Though I couldn't help but think that part, or most, of his resentment stemmed from his awkwardness in trying to manipulate his comparatively squat frame into the necessary positions.

But finally, the time came for our audience, and we were herded in front of two gigantic bronze doors. A gong sounded, and the doors began to open slowly of their own accord—probably due to some hidden mechanism. Frankly, the three of us were startled into breathlessness when the royal chamber doors were opened and there, beyond any doubt, was the supreme head of Asian Buddhism.

For a moment, we were stunned into a sort of paralysis, but soon enough we looked at one another as though deciding what we should do next. Then Sigme coughed loudly from the corridor outside and we began our entrance one by one, first Horace, then myself, and finally Sigerson.

When after a long while we were finally seated with our eyes averted, we heard the Most High's adolescent voice speak: "Mr. Holly, Mr. Vincey, Mr. Sigerson, I am very happy to see you." We were surprised by these, the first words we heard from the young man, who is, in effect, the Buddhist pope. "Please, don't let Brother Sigme's lessons intimidate you. I invite you to look at me."

We three looked up at once, and Horace, perhaps because he felt the wisest among us, rushed to speak next. "Your Highness, the pleasure is all ours, we assure you. Speaking for Leo and myself, we never expected to be honored by your presence during our sojourn here."

"You do yourselves an injustice," the High Lama said sternly, "and myself a disservice. I am neither completely rude nor are you representatives of distant empires completely below my notice. As for Mr. Sigerson, he is a special case; and it was inevitable that he… as a…er…an official representative of that esteemed nation Norway… would be welcome in my rooms."

Horace and I both looked at Sigerson with querying lifts of our eyebrows, for the reference to him left something to be desired, but he responded only with a shrug, then spoke to our host.

44

"Your Highness, you are supremely thoughtful as is expected and inevitable, for though you appear young in body, you measure your age not in years but in centuries . . . indeed, millennia . . ." (At this point Horace and I couldn't help but look at one another knowingly, for such a person—one who counted her years in this same fashion—we had known before) ". . . and your wisdom and compassion are correspondingly perfected."

Of course, here Sigerson was referring to the traditional Tibetan belief that each Dalai Lama is the latest incarnation of the previous Dalai Lama all the way back to Buddha himself. When a Dalai Lama dies, it is thought his spirit enters the body of a newborn boy, and monks search the country for a boy born the exact moment the High Lama stopped breathing. That baby is then taken to Lhasa and is raised to fulfill his destiny as the new Dalai Lama.

"It is so, but I did not have you brought here to exchange pleasantries. My uncle, the Regent, was perilously close to resorting to torture, and I thought it prudent to intervene lest such methods prove inadequate and your bodies be maimed to no avail. In fact, it was my hope that I could induce you to speak freely with an offer of gold, jewels, or other such trifles equal in sum to the value of the volume's cover, the acquisition of which was no doubt the reason you committed the crime to begin with."

"I'm sorry to disappoint you, Treasured King," Sigerson said quite calmly, "however, neither my friends nor myself have had any aspirations toward the item in question, and I'll repeat as I have many times before that we had nothing whatsoever to do with the murder or the theft."

"How am I supposed to believe that when all the evidence points clearly against you Europeans?"

Horace at this point spoke up. "Excuse me, Your Grace, but we have been accused and confined without being told a word about this so-called evidence. Exactly what is its nature so that we, too, can understand how it points so inexorably to us?"

"Certainly that is a fair question," the boy responded. He pulled a scrap of parchment from the fold in his robe that served as a pocket and referred to the document as he listed the evidence against us.

"First, near Paljori's body were found ashes of the noxious tobacco Mr. Sigerson enjoys so well. Second, in front of the cache where the sacred book was kept were footprints in the dust that only your European boots could have made. Thirdly, it is well known that your respective sojourns here in

Lhasa have been spent very nearly entirely in the said royal library. For what possible reason but to search for the sacred book and its jewel-encrusted cover? Fourth, it is well known that Europeans as a rule are mercenary, ruthless, and always liable to take the road that leads to riches when given the opportunity.

"My priests and I were lulled into an uncharacteristic letting down of our guard by Holly's and Vincey's talk of peculiar pillars and stone symbols, but rest assured, it won't happen again. Henceforth, our country will be absolutely closed to all non-Tibetans. There will be no exceptions. This will be so because I have said it!

"You sit before me and are accused, and you have heard the unassailable evidence against you. What have you to say?"

As the Dalai Lama spoke, I couldn't help but notice that Sigerson struggled to restrain himself from smiling. Apparently this was noticed by the High Lama as well, who said, "Mr. Sigerson, you find the facts amusing, I see."

"I only find amusing, sire, that so many good, intelligent men make so much of so little. A man trained in the powers of observation and reasoning could reach a far different conclusion from the same facts."

"Explain" The boy looked especially grim at that moment.

"Since no one actually saw the crimes in question, someone who wanted to put my friends and I under suspicion could easily have planted the evidence you listed. Do you truly think I am so stupid that I would empty my pipe at the site of a murder I've committed? Or leave incriminating footprints? No, Your Grace, we did not leave behind those clues . . . but I assure you that someone did."

"Who would you suggest?" the boy asked.

"That would be difficult to say without a thorough investigation, though I do have some ideas along those lines. Your Holiness, it so happens that in my professional duties in my home country I have dabbled in police work . . . investigations and such . . . and I have had some luck. You might say I have something of a knack in clearing up crimes. I beseech you now, if you are truly interested in finding both the guilty party and the missing tome, to take the shackles off me!"

The Dalai Lama was quiet for a time. We three merely stood before him. I for one felt rather foolish and was glad when the youth spoke again.

"Sigerson, I'm not sure why, but I am inclined to trust you—or rather, I'm not so stupid that I don't understand that if you three are executed, we may never find the sacred book. At least if you have a degree of mobility, you may lead us to the prize either out of carelessness or luck or skill. We will see what we will see."

"Your Grace, you will not regret this decision," said Sigerson.

"Naturally, however, your two friends must remain incarcerated to guarantee your reliability."

Horace and I both reacted sharply to the news. I don't think it is necessary to go into detail except to say I don't think I ever saw Horace so hot under the collar—the presence of His Holiness or not—except with the possible exception of his reaction to hearing the accusations against us some days earlier.

And, also, any idea that we might have had that we were alone with the Dalai Lama was quickly dispelled by the sudden appearance from around the entire perimeter of the room of a score of guards—who then vanished as rapidly as they appeared at a sign from the boy.

Sigerson, as to be expected, took both this news and the appearance of the guards with aplomb.

49

"Your Holiness," he said, "that would be inadvisable. I gather you wish to recover your property. I can guarantee that you will never see it again unless I aid you, and I will not aid you unless I can have the assistance of my two friends."

Well, you should have see the look on the young High Lama's face. It was rather as though he had just been informed that he had just ingested poison or had been bitten by a snake. The internal conflict wafted across his face: He was unsure whether to recall the guards and have us thrown into irons or to hold his royal temper and submit to Sigerson's demand. Fortunately, his last signal apparently had been a command to the effect that the guards leave the room entirely, for I'm sure that had any Tibetans been in attendance, the act of saving face would have been paramount and perhaps none of us would have seen another day. As it was, the young fellow seemed to count to ten, take a breath, look at Sigerson with renewed respect and finally say, "Your terms are difficult, Sigerson, but not impossible. You may have your assistants, but there will be three royal guards accompanying each of you at all times."

Sigerson smiled. "Agreed, Your Holiness. Capital!"

CHAPTER FOUR

The Dalai Lama's Story

As chaotic—almost dreamlike—as this whole episode seemed as we lived through it, the interview of the Dalai Lama by Sigerson that followed remains in my mind as the strangest, the most dreamlike. As I sat there in this Oriental hall on the far side of the world, surrounded by Golden Buddhas and all manner of alien accouterments, I watched Sigerson stretch out his long legs and steeple his hands below his thick beard, close his eyes and thereafter fasten on every word the boy uttered.

But here is the worst of the dream: As I watched the scene, I suddenly had the strongest impression of an English drawing room. I blinked and for a moment I thought I saw upright chairs with red velvet seats and backs, fine china set on a polished table, and newspapers scattered about. All during the interview, so long as Sigerson's eyes were closed and his attention was rapt on the Dalai Lama, I felt drawn to that room.

But that is neither here nor there; the things said by the boy should be the focus of this narrative at this point. The starting point of the Dalai Lama's story was Sigerson's query: "Pray tell me about the missing item and the circumstances of the death and theft."

That which follows is the boy's story. As you will see, it left much to be desired.

"Paljori was our honored and most revered librarian since the passing of Brother Tzu, Paljori's mentor, forty-five years ago. Part of Paljori's glory was—and this has never been mentioned to a non-Buddhist, non-Tibetan in millennia—was in the guarding of a holy book that has been handed down through many generations of librarians. The book itself is virtually worthless except for a few high lamas, for whom, of course, it is priceless. Its main value is its cover and box, or case, which are inlaid with gold and encrusted with jewels and are worth a fortune (from a Western perspective). But, what good are gold and jewels to a good Tibetan? None! That is why suspicion fell on you Europeans.

"What is your saying? It is worth a king's ransom. It's no wonder you would take it. But I forgot, in order for you to 'find' the missing item, I should not judge you in advance."

(You notice I felt it necessary to place find in quotation marks above. The reason is that the youngster's tone was such that he made it clear he never doubted our guilt.)

"However," he went on, "Brother Sun-Li, Paljori's apprentice, entered the library, as is his habit, two hours before dawn of the morning in question and found poor Paljori dead with a ceremonial sword through his heart. He was slumped over his prayer rug.

"Brother Sun-Li immediately told the first monk he encountered and in short time, Brother Wan-Po, our revered chief police monk, whom I believe you've met, was at the site of the murder. In short order, he had deduced the guilty parties . . . and the rest you know."

The Dalai Lama fell silent and observed the three of us with a kind of twinkle in his eye; I suppose because he considered the whole thing a game.

Well, my feeling about this is, if you make a child a god, then you have a childish god. But as has been mentioned before, the young Dalai Lama is not the real power; his powers are limited until he comes of age. My God! What if a fourteen-year-old boy became Prime Minister of England! Can you imagine it? It beggars the imagination!

But this aside is not pertinent to our situation, so I'll go on. Needless to say, our lives were in the young fellow's hands and any inclination toward mercy that he showed was appreciated. In fact, his show toward us was the only indication of mercy at all that had been granted us thus far. Despite his immaturity and his behavior with us, it was not he who had put us in this predicament. It was Brother Wan-Po.

Sigerson opened his eyes at the conclusion of the High Lama's tale and stood up abruptly.

"Well then, let us be on our way. I must see the scene of the crime. Call your guards or whoever you wish to accompany us. The game is afoot. Time is being wasted."

CHAPTER FIVE

The Monk of Long Ago

So it was that half an hour later, we were once again in the great Lhasa library with its thousands of ancient texts-one-time domain of the late Brother Paljori, Head Librarian.

Our nemesis, Wan-Po, was already there with his retinue. As we entered, I couldn't see that he was doing anything other than swaggering pompously hither and thither, his yellow robe swishing and his nose stuck in the air. It seemed probable that his presence was due to some messenger being sent out to inform him of our mission, and he saw fit to be there at our arrival, more to hinder us, I suppose, than to help us.

"The murderous Europeans, I see, come to obliterate the clues pointing to their guilt."

Sigerson would not be baited, however. He merely looked coldly at the rogue and asked, "Where precisely was the body found? In order to pursue my investigation I will need your cooperation. Tell me what you can, every detail you remember. This is by order of your most revered Dalai Lama."

Wan-Po didn't appear concerned by this information. Doubtlessly, he already had received word to the effect that Sigerson was to have his way. Wan-Po would obey his sovereign's command, but he wouldn't like it.

"So be it!" he said a bit too sweetly for my taste and shot to attention but not, as I said, with a bit of sincerity in his attitude. "Over there is the table at which Paljori sorted and catalogued new volumes as they arrived from the various monasteries of the realm. Beyond that is the alcove where he customarily prayed. There, slumped forward, a sword in his heart, his body was found."

Sigerson proceeded to the spot and surprised one and all by pulling a small magnifying glass out of a pocket, then, falling to his hands and knees, examining the floor and walls between the table and the alcove.

He occupied himself thus for about ten minutes, totally ignoring the varied sounds of consternation that emitted from Wan-Po, who grumbled and moaned and stamped his feet for the duration about his time being wasted and similar pointless concerns. I say pointless because the chap was such an inferior sort by any standard that, so far as I was concerned, Tibet would be better off if he found elsewhere to spend his time.

In any case, Sigerson was now examining the table and the books that were neatly piled at both ends.

"These books!" Sigerson shot. "Have they been moved since the incident?"

"All is as it was," Wan-Po replied. "Only Brother Paljori's remains have been removed."

Sigerson's reply was, "Harrumph!" Then he continued inspecting as before with his magnifying glass. Horace and I were dumbfounded by Sigerson's behavior. We spoke between ourselves and agreed that his mere physical presence and level of energy seemed to fill the place.

Finally he stood, turned abruptly to Wan-Po, and asked, "Where was your precious volume kept? A secret cache perhaps?"

The monk didn't seem to want to respond. He delayed his response sufficiently long that Sigerson made another noise of frustration.

"Are there exits, or doors, or rooms or other secret portals in the immediate vicinity?"

Wan-Po still didn't reply, though it appeared as though he was trying to say something. Finally, Sigerson stepped over to a shelf behind the table, where there were piled many long books with board covers from goodness knows when, reached behind and did something, and suddenly, a section of the wall adjacent swung open on a kind of hinge, revealing a passageway behind.

Wan-Po and all the other monks in attendance gasped in astonishment, then spoke rapidly amongst themselves. Wan-Po exclaimed, "More proof of your guilt! How would you know of the cache unless you had been here before when it was open . . . and stolen its contents?"

Sigerson didn't even honor this remark with a rebuff. He grabbed the nearest sweet-smelling butter lamp and crossed the threshold, glass in hand. We all made our way slowly down the passage, which was about forty feet long, following Sigerson. At the end was a wonderful room, a true secret chamber, hung with gold fabric and elaborate rugs and infinitely detailed paintings of historical scenes. As the lamp flickered, the metallic contents of the room sparkled, highlighting different quarters at different times. As interesting as the general ambiance of the room was, the nature of the scenes depicted in the paintings and rugs drew our special attention.

The main character was a Buddha-like figure, but not Buddha—that is to say, not the typical Buddha image. And the scenes were of this figure speaking to crowds. And there was another figure in attendance, a sort of compatriot to the thin Buddha.

Sigerson glanced around, didn't seem at all surprised by anything he saw, and stepped over to an elaborately carved wooden chest which was centered on a shelf along the back wall. He moved the chest aside and revealed a niche in the wall just big enough to hold a typical Tibetan book. Of course, it was empty.

Now Wan-Po positively gloated. "What more proof do I need?" he asked of those clustered in the small room. "With each passing minute, the man establishes his presence at the scene of the atrocious crime."

With admirable restraint, Sigerson continued to ignore the man's pompous remarks. Horace and I looked at one another as though to say, "My, my, he does seem more than passingly familiar with the layout of the place . . . ." Finally, after a few minutes of crawling around on the floor and peering into literally every corner of the room, Sigerson stood, positioned himself against a wall, folded his arms, and said, "Please, explain to me what this room held . . . in precise detail, if you will."

Wan-Po opened his mouth, with the intention of objecting, I'm certain, when Sigerson made a quick reference to the Dalai Lama, and the inspector monk groaned, and relayed the following history:

"For many centuries, a particular text, detailing the life of a beloved monk who lived long ago has been hidden in the very niche you see there. During the life and reign of each Dalai Lama, only three people at any given time know of its existence: the Dalai Lama, the head librarian whose duty it is to guard the text, and the chief of police monks.

"The text is of little importance except for ritual purposes; however, the boards that have covered the volume have over the centuries been inlaid with gold and decorated with jewels. It can't be imagined that the text was stolen for its own sake, but more likely for the value of the cover."

"Who was the monk whom you think so highly of?" Sigerson asked.

"His name was Issa. He lived long ago. It is said he knew Buddha himself, but that is only a story."

Sigerson mulled over what he had heard for a while, dropped his glass into his pocket, took one last look around and said, "I must see the body."

Wan-Po was taken aback by this. "Why, that is impossible. The vultures have taken him to heaven."

I suppose that for those uninitiated into the ways of Tibet that an explanation is due at this point. Because Tibet has little ground worthy of agriculture, most of it being rock, or rocky moraine, centuries ago the natives developed the pragmatic ritual known as "sky burial." It is simple enough: In lieu of ground to bury them in, each dawn undertakers chop to pieces the bodies of the recently deceased and feed them to carnivorous vultures, which Tibetans believe to be sacred beings that take the souls of the dead to paradise.

CHAPTER SIX

An Undertaker and a Doctor

Shortly thereafter, we found ourselves in the southeastern corner of Lhasa, where Sigerson sought to interview the "Disposers of the Dead," or morticians, at the sky burial site. Despite our familiarity with the subject, having tarried in Tibet at length, Horace and I exchanged glances of disgust. There had apparently been a "service" only recently, as there was a pool of blood in the middle of the clearing, and the air still smelled of the pine and cypress that was burnt to attract the vultures.

Wan-Po, who had belligerently accompanied us, spoke to one man explaining our mission. Sigerson, as might be gathered by now, was not one to waste time. He immediately introduced himself and began to fire a barrage of questions. He then took the undertaker aside by the arm and the two of them spoke in muffled voices for a time, the undertaker occasionally looking towards Wan-Po, as though seeking guidance, though not receiving any from the disgruntled monk.

While they spoke, I looked around. On three sides we were surrounded by gray outcroppings. A swarm of perhaps twenty-five vultures circled high overhead. Probably they had only just finished their meal as we had arrived.

Certainly, the vultures of Tibet are uncannily spoiled. Beyond what I've explained in passing, there are also these details to share, gentle reader: Following the dissection of the corpse, the first thing the undertaker does is remove and pound the bones, mixing them with tsampa-roasted barley flour. This mixture is fed to the vultures first. In this way, no mortal remains are left. Once every morsel of the corpse is devoured, the birds take flight. The soul is set free.

Finally Sigerson grunted approval and ventured back to our group.

"Capital!" He seemed to actually gloat. "Now I must see Paljori's rooms!"

Paljori, it proved, lived in a small one room apartment adjoining his precious library.

Wan-Po showed us through with a contemptuous bow. Sigerson proceeded as before, instantly taking command, bustling about, glass in hand, peering in every corner, crevice, and crack. The room itself was similar to other monks' rooms,

63

so far as I could see, which is to say, it was identical in sparseness.

We were there about five minutes when Sigerson rushed through the opening that served as a door and demanded of Wan-Po to see the chief medical monk. Once again we traveled the breadth of the city, and we were introduced to Brother Linga, the very fellow who helped diagnosis Horace's heart condition. The meeting proved to be the twin of the one with the mortician—hushed whispers out of earshot.

Finally Sigerson came back to our group and told all present that he would like to spend a quiet evening with Horace and myself in his rooms, and that in the morning he would announce who, without doubt, the murderer was and also locate the missing priceless tome.

CHAPTER SEVEN

Sigerson's Solutions

So it was that we three Europeans found ourselves in comparative comfort for the first time in several days, albeit with guards stationed in the hall outside Sigerson's door. Truth to tell, we were all exhausted. For the life of me, I couldn't imagine how Sigerson could be so confident that he'd solved the riddle, when I certainly saw nothing that pointed in any direction other than toward ourselves.

During the hours that preceded our retiring for the night, Horace and I engaged Sigerson in an intellectual debate, the point of which was Horace trying to knock Sigerson off his high horse. However, Sigerson maintained his irritatingly haughty attitude, and there was nothing for Horace and I to do but hope that tomorrow would be a better day.

Yet, part of me believes (in retrospect, mind you) that Sigerson was terribly lonely that night. We were invited to his room to share time with him, but his attitude rubbed us the wrong way and distanced us. I wonder, in light of later events, how that night would have gone if Horace and I had been more agreeable and open to the man. Perhaps it was we—faced with the unbelievable—who were rude and insensitive, and not he, who was merely justifiably proud of his abilities. A man looking back on his life often regrets decisions, and wishes he could reverse some—this is one of those times for me.

Regardless, the following describes our discussion that night:

When we were settled down, Sigerson on his rough bed, Horace on what passed for a chair, and myself on the dirt floor, Sigerson asked, "Well, what do you think? Did I run these rascals ragged? Do you have any ideas?"

Horace said, "Frankly, Sigerson, I have to admit I'm impressed with the energy expended in your efforts; however, I'm at a loss to understand what you could have possibly learned. A lot of chasing after wild gooses if you ask me."

Sigerson laughed, which, of course, may as well have been calculated to set off poor Horace. Whatever else Sigerson does or doesn't have, or can or cannot do, I can say with assurance that his social graces leave much to be desired. I never knew a man who could so easily upset all those around him with a mere flick of the wrist or toss of the head or a slightly-off tone of voice.

But before Horace could even open his mouth to object, I jumped in, stating, "Well, it's all still a mystery to me. What could those horrid vulture feeders have been able to tell you, or for that matter, how could the dust in the corners of the rooms have made any difference? I only pray that we can get out of this with our skins."

"My feeling," continued Horace, "is that there is more here than meets the eye. I don't believe that you are what you say you are, Sigerson. So out with it. Who are you? What are you doing here? What is all this hocus-pocus you've been trying to pass off as deduction and detection—?"

"My good man! Holly, I dare say, please. You are getting yourself overwrought! You yourself speak of 'more than meeting the eye.' My avocation is simply spying those details—sometimes remarkable, sometimes not—that nine hundred ninety-nine people out of a thousand don't see. The details are there, sometimes blown into corners by draughts, sometimes as isolated bits of information taken for granted by one person but not even known to another. I look for all these disparate pieces and assemble them. Sometimes the process is simple, like pieces of a puzzle neatly coming together, and voilà, there is the answer! Other times, the solution is more difficult to ascertain." "Skullduggery is more like it!"

"Horace, honestly, I, too, am beginning to lose my patience with your fears. The man has just successfully bought us some time. We need now to plan our escape."

"Perhaps, as a fallback, that is a good idea," Sigerson offered. "However, if we can accept the word of the high lamas here, we will be able to walk away tomorrow, if such is our desire."

"How can you possibly say that?"

"Obviously, I'll simply tell them who killed Paljori and lead them to their sacred book. When they have everything they want, they will release us."

"Do you mean to say you actually know these things?"

"Of course."

The absurdity of it struck me as funny. Therefore, I knew what Horace's feelings must be. I had to hurry to think of an idea to circumvent his wrath.

"Well, then, let us try to guess the answer," I ventured. "We were with you today, saw nearly everything you saw, met the people you met. I know I have a theory, as must Horace. Let's compare our ideas."

"Capital!"

"I believe there are Chinese spies among us." "Now, why on earth would you think that?"

"Well, obviously since the Dalai Lama is involved, it must be some big political brouhaha, which indicates international intrigue. At present, there are only three nations interested in Tibet from a political point of view—Britain, Russia, and China. Holly and I are the only representatives of Her Majesty here, and we are certainly not spies, let alone killers. That leaves the Russians and the Chinese. But since there has been no evidence of non-Orientals lurking about, then the culprit or culprits must be Chinese disguised as Tibetans."

"Most impressive, Vincey. Yes, yes, a most impressive feat of mental derring-do. Unfortunately, you could not be further from the truth."

"And why do you say that?"

"Well, for one thing, the Russians could easily have utilized Mongolians, or border Tibetans for that matter, but it is a more fundamental problem than that. What about you, Holly?"

"Frankly, it is as much a mystery to me today as it was when we first heard about it. I don't see where it all leads. I only hope we get out of this fix somehow. In fact, I hope that you are right in whatever it is you reveal tomorrow, Sigerson."

"So be it!"

We retired late that night and slept restlessly. Indeed, I think that sleep was denied Horace entirely, for I would awaken intermittently through the night and hear my foster father muttering to himself.

But at last, the guards roused us the next morning and off we went to confront Wan-Po in the temple. There was some arguing between him and Sigerson, then the Norwegian suggested we all return to Paljori's apartment, which we did in short order.

"Wan-Po, please give me a description of the book."

"It is two feet long, perhaps four inches thick, and eight wide. The cover boards are the rarest mahogany inlaid with gold, emeralds, rubies, diamonds. This ornamentation was created centuries ago in the form of a dragon eating its own tail by a master artisan of such high caliber the world has never seen another like him. The pages are a kind of parchment, brittle now and so brown the text is barely discernible."

"Admirable. Admirable, indeed."

Just at this point, without so much as a whisper to warn us of his approach, and with a grand flourish consisting of piercing tones from six-foot-long ceremonial horns, conch shells, various reed instruments, and drums, the young Dalai Lama entered the room. It was a most unexpected and awesome entrance.

"Excuse me, gentlemen, but I was curious," said the boy.

Sigerson's eyes glowed with fire. "Ah, you are just in time, Your Grace!" he said triumphantly.

And then with a dramatic turn, Sigerson thrust aside Paljori's rough cot and pointed at a section of the wall.

"There is where you will find your precious document." Astonished, I peered at what he was pointing to, but could only see the blank wall. The others in the room appeared equally confused.

"What manner of nonsense is this?" Wan-Po erupted. "Do you take me for a fool?"

"Humour me, my good man, and touch that section of wall and then the surrounding sections."

Reluctantly, the Dalai Lama's head police officer did so.

"This section is rougher than the surrounding areas. So what?"

"I do believe that if you were to set men to gouge out a hole at that spot, you'll find your document."

Not to drag out this narrative longer than necessary, they did just that, and, as God is my witness, in a cache in the wall, wrapped in the finest silks, was the book in question, housed in a box and between covers every bit as fine as we'd been led to believe.

Horace groaned and whispered to me, "Don't you see it? Sigerson was the guilty party all the time. How else would he have known where to look? He is the murderer. And how clever he is to have hidden it where no one else in the world would have dreamt to look for it."

I looked at Horace with horror. I couldn't believe he actually believed what he said. To my mind, however idiosyncratic Sigerson might sometimes seem, he wouldn't have allowed us to be falsely accused. No. It was unthinkable!

Sigerson, for his part, though he must have heard Horace's frustrated remark, chose to ignore it, and instead confronted Wan-Po. The police monk was tenderly looking over the volume when Sigerson interjected. "You have your volume now, and I can safely presume that it is in fact the tome for which you were so desperate, not the elaborate cover and box. Gold and jewels are replenishable; whatever this manuscript may be, is not."

Wan-Po ignored Sigerson's statement and looked up with suspicion in his eyes. Then he made, in his own language, a remark nearly identical to Horace's, denouncing Sigerson as the ultimate culprit.

"On the contrary. 'Twas not I," Sigerson calmly responded. "But I know who is, or was, rather."

We waited. All eyes inevitably drifted to the Dalai Lama's expectant expression.

Sigerson drew out the moment, slowly meeting the gaze of each and every person present. For a moment, I felt I was immersed in a stage production. Finally, he spoke again.

"Paljori was deathly afraid of Vincey there, and Holly and myself—for no other reason than we represented the different. But worse than his fear of us as individuals, he feared what we represented—our homelands, the Western world, our governments. He could not allow us to leave your country to report, so that others would follow us. There was no greater threat in the world to the man, and he plotted how to be rid of us. He needed for us to enrage those Tibetans who had the power to triple and quadruple the civil effort to prevent foreigners from penetrating your borders. He had to guarantee that no non-Tibetan would ever again enter Tibet, let alone travel all the way to Lhasa."

I realized my jaw was hanging open. Horace, I saw, was pale.

"Paljori, gentlemen, hid the book himself where he felt no one would ever look, planted evidence that pointed clearly and irrevocably to my friends and myself, then simply killed himself. His faith in his convictions was so great."

Wan-Po was too taken aback to speak.

"Proof? You will want proof for such an apparently outlandish conclusion, of course," Sigerson continued. "I can quickly provide it. Will the undertaker and the medical monk, who are waiting outside, please step in?"

Whereupon the two indicated persons stepped in from outside, clearly uncomfortable to be in the presence of their revered spiritual leader on one hand, and to be the centers of attention on the other.

"You'll have to excuse this little surprise," Sigerson went on. "Your Grace, you'll remember, you gave me the power to question these men. I took the liberty, as well, to ask them to be available here at this time. Now, I'll have them clear up this last sticky point."

Whereupon, in response to queries from Sigerson, the medical monk described the nature of the wound, as did the mortician, both indicating that the slash was just deep enough to have been inflicted by the wielder of the sword in question, but not so deep as one would expect if a second person had wielded the weapon.

Finally, Wan-Po was convinced, as was Horace. The Dalai Lama was clearly impressed.

As a reward, Sigerson asked only that we three foreigners be given the opportunity to learn the contents of the document that was so important to our hosts and so nearly disastrous for us.

The boy granted Sigerson's request. Unexpectedly, the volume proved to be written in Aramaic. Horace, being familiar with the written form of the language, volunteered to read it aloud. Though there was Tibetan annotation, he read directly from the original. I wish to God he hadn't read it at all. But it is not mine to pick or choose as God might. Here is a copy of the old Tibetan book. Make of it as you will.

The Gospel of Issa

1. Is it God or is it I who guides this brush? God fills me as milk warm from the goat fills a cup to overflowing.

2. Long ago I ceased to be merely the man who is the son of my parents. I was young when God showed Himself to me:

3. That was the time I ceased to be the son of my parents. I became then an instrument of the Lord. I, Issa, son of Joseph, the carpenter of Nazareth, ceased to be.

4. My whole will from that time forward focused on the fact of God's gracing me with the indisputable awareness of His presence.

5. Why me? What did I ever do to deserve the acquaintance of God? My time and my life have been for these last eighteen years fully a matter of trying to understand what was and is happening to me.

6. I am filled with God. But tell me, if you empty a fig of its meat and fill its skin with mandarin orange pulp, are you left with an orange?

7. Then I am no more God than the fig is an orange. But as that fig, transformed, knows more of oranges than a natural fig, so I know more of God than a natural man.

8. They will say, I think, that I am the son of God. Others will say I am a fraud!

9. I know that the Lord has chosen me for some other than ordinary purpose. I can see glimpses of it, but the details elude me.

10. These things are fact, not to be ignored by me or anyone.

11. I know clearly how the prophets must have felt; what they must have known. As God spoke to Abraham and Moses and Isaiah, so He speaks to me.

12. I truly know that I am to do my Lord's bidding; I am to be the instrument of His will.

13. My Lord wants me to wander through the East and absorb everything I see and hear.

14. So be it. Such is what we have done for nearly eighteen years. Here I am with my brother Didymus Judas Thomas in the land of the Bon,* the mightiest mountain country that my Father has created.

15. We have traveled far, about as far from home as is imaginable.

16. I have learned much: the tenets of Hinduism, Buddhism, Confucianism, yoga. These are all fonts from which I have drunk mightily.

17. What is it now that I am supposed to do? Is it time to return? Home has beckoned for months now.

---

* Editor's note: An ancient name for Tibet.—T.K.M.

18. Is there anything else to learn in this high land of false magic and superstition? Will I know what to do when the time comes?

19. Now, however, I write this account as You have asked, or, rather, ordered, for my Father does not ask.

20. I am here, Lord; but I don't know why. I have learned much, but I don't know why. We have traveled far, and I don't know why.

21. Everything is so different than that which I was taught as a child in Nazareth.

22. Is it that I am loath to admit to myself what your purpose is for me?

23. In our wanderings, I have noted a common theme. A tenet that explains so much—that answers so many of your children's unanswered questions.

24. Whether in China or India or here in the loftiest mountains, so long as I am in the East, I hear of death and

rebirth, and of the soul using the body much as I would ride in a vehicle:

25. How after death, the soul must be born again. Though in a new vehicle, or vessel, according to the merit that the soul exhibited in its previous existences.

26. It is a meritorious approach to existence certainly. Much as a school boy moves from one level of learning to another higher level, so, too, a death marks the potential for a move, for the coming to a crossroads;

27. But as some children need to repeat an entire season of lessons due to slothfulness or poor behavior or inattentiveness, so, too, a soul must sometimes repeat a wasted life in order to attain the merit to move on.

28. Attainment of merit is simple, surely. To do onto others as you would have them do onto you.

29. If a man or a woman follows this tenet for a lifetime, he or she will achieve merit and be closer to God for having done so: In this life and in the next.

30. To be One with the Father, that is the purpose of existence: base man must rise above his baseness to sit at the right hand of the Father.

31. Yet it is slow. God's time is not man's time, nor woman's. A human lifetime is but the single beat of a fly's wing in God's measure.

32. The miracle is that God notices, and more than this, that God cares.

33. But God does care. If God was not Love Incarnate, perhaps all of human existence could have begun and ended without the Father even knowing.

34. But God does know and God does love.

35. Patience is the foundation.

36. An hour, a day, a month, a year, seven years, a single lifetime is not enough.

37. I have had arguments, or, rather, discussions with my brother Thomas.

38. It is self-apparent, I will say to him, that the punishment for the curser is that the soul will forget its previous life and will be cast down into a body that will spend its time continually troubled in its heart;

39. That the punishment for the arrogant and over-bearing man is that the soul will forget from whence it came and will be cast down into a lame and deformed body so that all despise it persistently.

40. Then Thomas will ask, "And the man who hath committed no sin, but done good persistently, but hath not found the mysteries, what will happen to him?"

41. And I reply, "He will seek the light and will find it."

42. Surely, then, my destiny is to teach of these matters and others, such as the righteousness of humility and

of seeking and others of which I have learned during our long sojourn.

43. But to whom? Surely, the people of our fathers, the people of Abraham will make naught of such matters.

44. Oh, my brother and I have seen so much in these last years.

45. By caravan, we followed the silk road to Bactra and from thence to Kabul and Palitara. I have seen the holy cities of Juggernaut, Rajagrina, Benares, and Kopilavastu.

46. We have journeyed through many nations and supped with many peoples.

47. I am filled to overflowing with the wisdom of the ages.

48. You told me that I am Your tool. Well, use me! I have much knowledge and have acquired marvelous techniques. What is it all for? I am tired.

49. (Could it be that it was I who wrote here of patience?)

50. I know now that I am to teach. Well, then, let me teach! How much more must I learn? I have seen your many faces!

51. Eloi, Eloi! I am lonely. Despite the companionship of my brother, Thomas, I am tired of being a stranger in a strange land.

52. I have learned without doubt that You are Love, but I do not love. I have teachers but no friends.

53. I am feeling sorry for myself, for I am lonely and too wise.

54. I know God as well as I know Joseph, the husband of my mother, Mariam.

55. In the beginning, when I was very young, He would speak to me, and I would respond.

56. He spoke to me and it was clear enough. Not in words would He speak, but in signs and symbols and, sometimes, in dreams, too, He made His wants known. Learning the language of the signs was the challenge.

57. What is school if not a challenge for the student?

58. As a child who does good is rewarded, and is punished for having done bad, so, too, God shows pleasure when a sign is read correctly and displeasure when a sign is misread.

59. Usually some coincidence that inspired wonder would be my reward for right interpretation; a sense of foreboding being the clue that there was misreading.

60. I needed always to plumb my feelings and try to understand what God was trying to say. In time, I built a whole vocabulary.

***

61. My brother, Issa, is dead. I, Didymus Judas Thomas, who has been my brother's companion for nearly eighteen years as we traveled through the strange lands of the East, am now alone. I am afraid. God has deserted us.

62. Issa was attacked in a dark alley by robbers and was clubbed to death. The morticians here, who feed their dead to the birds, have him in their care now.

63. I cannot bear to stay in this foreign land one day longer. I am leaving for home, Judea.

64. I have much to carry; I leave behind much; my burdens are heavy.

[Thus ends the manuscript.]

Conclusion

Horace was silent for a time, as we all were. Eventually, he seemed to awaken as from a trance and carefully picked up the loose leaves he had been turning over as he read, straightened them neatly, and replaced them onto the back cover, then replaced the top board, effectively returning the volume to the state in which we found it.

Then Horace folded his hands over the book and bent his head. I think he was praying. Sigerson was sitting with his back against the wall, his hands steepled as he so often held them, and appeared in deep concentration.

The young Dalai Lama, to whom, presumably, the story was familiar, sat calmly on Paljori's cot watching us passively.

For myself, I felt dazed, confused—only dimly aware of the impressions I've recorded above.

Finally, Horace looked up. I saw a hopeful glow on his countenance.

"Issa died here in Tibet," he said. "Obviously what we are all thinking . . . must be a case of mistaken identity. The man we've known as Jesus and this Issa must not have been the same man, since Jesus continued to live for some years."

Before anyone could respond directly, a thought suddenly loomed in my mind. I suppose my face must have registered some sort of shock for suddenly all eyes in that room were upon me.

The thought was so startling that I didn't want to speak it aloud. But I saw I had no choice.

"There is a conclusion that naturally follows from the narrative we have just heard: If the real Jesus of Nazareth died here in Tibet, then someone claiming to be him appeared in Palestine sometime afterward. This brings up the possibility of an impersonator."

"My God," said Horace. "That can't be! For that would mean that all of Christianity is based on the work of an impostor. Could the entire faith of the Western world be predicated on a sham? No, by God!"

No one in the room responded.

Horace continued, "No, Leo. You forget, when Jesus returned, he was accepted by his family, by his mother, and by Thomas his brother, who apparently was the last to see him, at least according to this narrative."

To which I said, "Jesus left the fold when he was twelve. Eighteen years later, a man returned claiming to be

Jesus. An imposter, I believe, could have s

perpetrated this fraud under those circumstances."

"But what about Thomas?" Horace cou

would have been in the best position to recogni

and didn't . . . ."

Horace's voice faded. Surely he remem

was, in fact, Thomas who was the most vocal wit

All this time Sigerson maintained his

Horace finally demanded of him, "Well, man,

think?"

Sigerson put down his pipe. "Yes, y

think indeed? I think we've heard all that i

deduce the truth. It is straightforward. Issa sper

India where he no doubt was a disciple of H

became adept at controlling his respiration, t

pulse, and when he was attacked by the hoc

chance to escape, he feigned death to avoid a

Thomas, who was not privy to the extent

spiritual prowess, in low spirits quit the East

returned home.

"Following his brother's departure, I

roused himself from his self-induced trai

...mself alone, continued his adventures and education for a ...le time, and then he, too, returned."

Horace closed his eyes tightly, then opened them and ...ke: "You're saying that Jesus made himself appear to die, ...n sometime later awakened and continued his business."

"Yes."

"Then, assuming what you say has some basis in truth, ...t which he accomplished once, he could accomplish again, ...ldn't he?"

Sigerson didn't reply, merely sucking on the pipe that ...l pulled out and lit at some point. The young Dalai Lama ...se this moment to interject his thoughts.

"Gentlemen, it is quite clear, I think, that the results of ...investigation, if taken in a certain light, could be the death ...l of your Christianity. It is my understanding that belief in ...s' resurrection is the foundation of your faith. Take away ...rection and suddenly there is no foundation. If your Jesus ...ot in fact come back from the dead, but pretended to—"

"No, no! Don't say it, Your Grace! I cannot bear to ...t."

Horace was beside himself with grief. For myself, I ...l with confusion. What did it all mean? Could Jesus ...: have been a fraud? Was he a mere charlatan who

90

successfully duped half the world, and all of Western civilization? Could all sanctity and piety be nothing more than a joke? Sigerson must have read the thoughts on my face. Certainly Horace was as pale as a ghost. I doubted I looked better.

"Now see here, men, straighten up," Sigerson said.

Whereas to this point he had maintained his smug, self-satisfied posture, for once he became thoroughly serious. He knocked his pipe out onto the dirt floor and drew Horace and I close.

"Now the way I see it," he said, "Issa, or Jesus, was not a fraud—was hardly a villain—and was every bit as good a man as we all take him to be—but he was a victim of circumstances. I believe he eventually returned to his home where he reestablished himself in his family and began to share his acquired wisdom with his neighbors. As word got around about this man and his radical views, people flocked to him and he found himself thrown into the position of teacher.

"Doubtless, he had no intention of dying before his time, and when he found himself arrested and condemned, he realized that he had within himself the means to survive. Whether or not he planned to be discovered walking about later, it is hard to say. But he was spotted and, no matter his explanation, to the great unwashed of Palestine his continued existence seemed a miracle.

"Poor Jesus, I'm sure he would be appalled to learn that what was likely an act of self-preservation has been misinterpreted through the ages."

Horace and I didn't feel much relieved after hearing this. Perhaps Jesus wasn't a fraud per se, but the alternative proposed by Sigerson nevertheless toppled the pillars and shattered the foundations of Christianity.

The Dalai Lama spoke again: "It seems so strange that a misunderstanding could root itself and become so integral a part of a faith for millennia."

"Your Grace, you should well know why the concept of resurrection has held for so long. It was because there was, after all, some basis of truth in it."

For myself, after having had my soul, my very identity as a Christian, dashed to the ground, this little bit of news seemed to hold succor. I waited hopefully.

"After all, resurrection is merely a form of rebirth. And it was a different doctrine of rebirth that Jesus no doubt shared with his people. It is clear, I think, what Jesus' message was when he returned from the East. Jesus saw his people suffering under the Roman yoke and shared with them the laws of karma. He taught them to do onto others as they would have them et cetera. Seek and you will find.

"Quite clearly, within the remnants of his thoughts that have been preserved to the present, these notions are paramount. He taught that to do good was all important and that, whether or not they were rewarded in this life, they would be in the next. These are clearly karmic concepts.

"But it appears that following the delivery of his message, much was lost, forgotten, misinterpreted, deleted, changed, appended, and amended; still, doubtless a fair number of references to karma and metempsychosis still existed. But even those—all but a few fragmentary references such as those I just indicated—were purged from all Christian writings after 553 A.D."

"Why 553 A.D.?" I asked petulantly.

"It is rather a convoluted story. I will see if I can summarize it: Our orthodox versions of the New Testament date no further back than that year, when the Byzantine Emperor Justinian called the Fifth Ecumenical Congress of Constantinople in 553 A.D., supposedly to condemn the writings of a certain early church father.

"During that congress, events were initiated that caused the relatively few Bibles then extant to be edited or destroyed and all competitive gospels and histories of Christ to be likewise destroyed. This appears to be largely the doing of Justinian's Empress, Theodora, who, it is said, started out as an actress and prostitute. How a commoner became an empress is another story. Suffice it to say she was world-wise and greed-driven, and she beguiled Justinian. Before long she was running the Empire as Justinian sniveled at her side.

"It was Theodora's great hope that upon her death, she would be instantly elevated to divine status. Since the doctrine of metempsychosis, with its slow cycles of birth and rebirth, opposed such an immediate destiny for her, she set about obliterating every reference to that doctrine that existed in the Empire and beyond. The fact that Christ's very teachings contradicted her desire did not matter. There was a conflagration that lasted decades as books were burnt across the civilized world. Thus nearly all references to Christ's Eastern teachings were deleted from the bible or altered to reflect a view that did not offend the Emperor and Empress. The latter, by the way, died in 547, six years before the congress in question. Apparently Justinian was determined that his consort would get her way posthumously.

"Beyond this, you must remember that the various books of the New Testament were pieced together totally independently of one another from a potpourri of pieces and sources. God only knows what was lost before Justinian and Theodora did their damage!"

Horace and I listened to all this sullenly. What were we to say? What further comment could we make? Sigerson spoke again. He said, "I live by a philosophy that has done good service for me. Namely, when all possibilities have been eliminated and all that is left is the impossible, then the impossible is the solution.

"Frankly, it appears obvious to me that metempsychosis is the only logical solution to the great mystery of the Injustice of Life—how it is that the good are allowed to suffer while the wicked roll in blessings, that innocent children should die, that plagues devastate populations and war destroys all. Otherwise Life on earth is a travesty . . . otherwise Life on earth is a mockery . . . otherwise Life on earth has no meaning at all."

"But how could God," I was prompted to ask, "have allowed the Bible to be so tampered with?"

"Because," Sigerson shot back, "though altered and watered down, it still served His purpose: The vision of Christ's resurrection and the festival of Easter still gave people hope—and certainly Christianity taught that we're all responsible for our actions. The root moral concepts underlying metempsychosis were still there, just obscured. The altered message still served God's plan."

And so it continued until I was numb with exhaustion. And finally there came a time when we all retired to our respective quarters.

**

Once we were back in the solitude and quiet of our apartment, thoughts came without my prompting:

Were we to accept reincarnation in place of Christ's resurrection? Certainly, I, Leo Vincey, of all people, had something to say in the matter! Am I not—even now—searching for a woman—my true love—who I know beyond a doubt is dead, for I saw her die with my own eyes? Isn't it true that Horace and I are searching for Ayesha's new incarnation, though we've never gone so far to admit it quite in that fashion before? Didn't she claim that I myself was the reincarnation of one Kallikrates, an Egyptian priest? Certainly, during our encounter with Ayesha, I believed none of her stories; but now I ask myself time and again, if I don't believe, why then am I searching for her now? Why have I spent six good years of my life looking for her who has already died? I suppose I must believe in my heart, or these last many years have been a waste!*

Then again, even if I were to admit belief in reincarnation, does that necessarily mean that Jesus had anything at all to do with the doctrine? Does that invalidate resurrection? What does my belief or disbelief have to do with Jesus and the birth of Christianity?

So many questions. So much muddle in my mind. I have no answers.

It was shortly after his reading of the sacred text that Horace fell ill. I believe the foundations of all that he believed in were battered irreparably. Can I blame Sigerson? Part of me wishes we never met the man with his cold insufferable logic. Yet part of me is also aware that Horace and I shared a fabulous adventure with the man. I hold nothing against him. We all must do what we must do.

So I have done what I set out to do; I have recorded an incident that might have been better left unrecorded. Still I

---

* Editor's note: Ten more years will pass before Leo and Horace find Ayesha.—T.K.M.

could not sit back and pretend it didn't happen. Horace and I will linger here in Lhasa until he recovers sufficiently to continue our trek, or return home, whichever seems appropriate at the time. Sigerson is preparing to leave—in search of Yeti he says. I wish him luck.

There is nothing more to tell.

L.V

Addendum

Upon returning to Lhasa three months after the incident last recorded in this narrative—from an interesting and hardly fruitless quest into the Nepalese Himalayas—I was given the Vincey journal by His Holiness the High Lama, who said Vincey left it with the request that I deal with it as I saw fit, or for the fates to deal with it as they will if I had no interest in it.

I note that Vincey did an adequate job of relating the circumstances and facts much as I recall them, though it is odd to read of another's sentiments toward oneself. Be that as it may, I will take this journal back to England, where I'm sure Watson will be interested in it, and possibly arrange through his or Holly's agent to have it published as a worthy footnote to Holly's and Vincey's original adventures.

It should be noted here, therefore, for the benefit of those who will not be content until they understand the reasoning, how it was I knew where to find the hidden latch that worked the secret door opening onto the chamber of Issa's journal. It is really very simple. We know that the library—which is contemporaneous with the Potala Palace— is many centuries old and that many generations of librarians have guarded the volume, checking it probably daily. In point of fact, the stone floor had been worn down over this period by the countless tread of librarians' feet so that a wide, shallow groove led right to the latch, and, similarly, the stone hollow where the latch was hidden was worn smooth and shone brightly as a result of myriad handlings.

Notwithstanding the above, I—*

---

* Editor's note: Here the manuscript ends. One can't help but wonder why "Sigerson" did not in fact carry the journal back to England with him, since its coming into my possession via Nepal would indicate the notebooks remained behind. Perhaps Holmes had a change of heart. Or perhaps they were stolen from him by Nepalese highwaymen. Regardless, we of our time and our heirs must be grateful that "the fates" saw fit that these pages eventually fell into sympathetic hands.—T. K. M.

Acknowledgments

One of the two mysteries in this story came to mind partly as the result of a conversation almost 40 years ago with a university acquaintance who suggested—while we raced madly in a cluttered college journalism pressroom "to put to bed" an issue of the *Phoenix*—that Jesus might have had some dealings with yogis.

Works by Nicholas Notovitch, Joseph Head and S.L. Cranston, T. Lobsang Rampa, Noel Langley, and Morton Cohen, among others, provided invaluable research material in the form of color, inspiration, and insight. Randy Cassingham provided several copy-editing suggestions.

I like to think that H. Rider Haggard and Arthur Conan Doyle, Knights of the Realm both, approve of this effort, wherever they may be.

About the Author

Thomas Kent Miller (often known as Thos. Kent Miller) is author of *Mars in the Movies: A History* (2016) from McFarland publishers, and the three Holmes/Haggard pastiches that comprise this "Holmes Behind the Veil" series.

Visit my Sherlock Holmes memoir-style blog: https://sherlockholmesmeetsallanquatermain.blogspot.com— the story of the writing of one novel. I also maintain a colorful interactive *Mars in the Movies: A History* blog: http://marsinthemoviesahistory.blogspot.com.

I am a member of The Friends of Arthur Machen and The Rider Haggard Society. I have written for *The Weird Tales Collector, The Ghosts & Scholars M. R. James Newsletter, Faunus: The Journal of the Friends of Arthur Machen, The Haggard Journal, Wormwood*, Borgo Press, Wildside Press, HarperCollins San Francisco, and Hippocampus Press.

My interests include science-fiction movies, Victorian and Edwardian ghost stories, 19th-century Hudson River School landscape paintings, and home theater. I live in southern California, and I can be contacted at: thomaskentmiller@gmail.com.

Also from MX Publishing

MX Publishing is the world's largest specialist Sherlock Holmes publisher, with over a hundred titles and fifty authors creating the latest in Sherlock Holmes fiction and non-fiction.

From traditional short stories and novels to travel guides and quiz books, MX Publishing cater for all Holmes fans.

The collection includes leading titles such as *Benedict Cumberbatch In Transition* and *The Norwood Author* which won the 2011 Howlett Award (Sherlock Holmes Book of the Year).

MX Publishing also has one of the largest communities of Holmes fans on Facebook with regular contributions from dozens of authors.

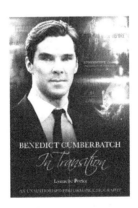

www.mxpublishing.com

Also from MX Publishing

  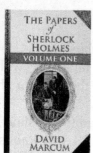

Our bestselling books are our short story collections;

'Lost Stories of Sherlock Holmes' , 'The Outstanding Mysteries of Sherlock Holmes', The Papers of Sherlock Holmes Volume 1 and 2, 'Untold Adventures of Sherlock Holmes' (and the sequel 'Studies in Legacy) and 'Sherlock Holmes in Pursuit', 'The Cotswold Werewolf and Other Stories of Sherlock Holmes' – and many more......

  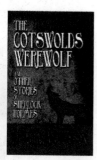

www.mxpublishing.com

Also from MX Publishing

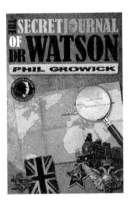

"Phil Growick's, 'The Secret Journal of Dr Watson', is an adventure which takes place in the latter part of Holmes and Watson's lives. They are entrusted by HM Government (although not officially) and the King no less to undertake a rescue mission to save the Romanovs, Russia's Royal family from a grisly end at the hand of the Bolsheviks. There is a wealth of detail in the story but not so much as would detract us from the enjoyment of the story. Espionage, counter-espionage, the ace of spies himself, double-agents, double-crossers...all these flit across the pages in a realistic and exciting way. All the characters are extremely well-drawn and Mr Growick, most importantly, does not falter with a very good ear for Holmesian dialogue indeed. Highly recommended. A five-star effort."
The Baker Street Society

www.mxpublishing.com

Also from MX Publishing

The Missing Authors Series

Sherlock Holmes and The Adventure of The Grinning Cat
Sherlock Holmes and The Nautilus Adventure
Sherlock Holmes and The Round Table Adventure

"Joseph Svec, III is brilliant in entwining two endearing and enduring classics of literature, blending the factual with the fantastical; the playful with the pensive; and the mischievous with the mysterious. We shall, all of us young and old, benefit with a cup of tea, a tranquil afternoon, and a copy of Sherlock Holmes, The Adventure of the Grinning Cat."
Amador County Holmes Hounds Sherlockian Society

www.mxpublishing.com

Also from MX Publishing

The American Literati Series

 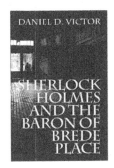 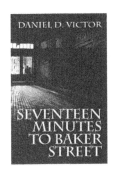

The Final Page of Baker Street
The Baron of Brede Place
Seventeen Minutes To Baker Street

"The really amazing thing about this book is the author's ability to call up the 'essence' of both the Baker Street 'digs' of Holmes and Watson as well as that of the 'mean streets' of Marlowe's Los Angeles. Although none of the action takes place in either place, Holmes and Watson share a sense of camaraderie and self-confidence in facing threats and problems that also pervades many of the later tales in the Canon. Following their conversations and banter is a return to Edwardian England and its certainties and hope for the future. This is definitely the world before The Great War."
Philip K Jones

www.mxpublishing.com

Also from MX Publishing

The Detective and The Woman Series

The Detective and The Woman
The Detective, The Woman and The Winking Tree
The Detective, The Woman and The Silent Hive

"The book is entertaining, puzzling and a lot of fun. I believe the author has hit on the only type of long-term relationship possible for Sherlock Holmes and Irene Adler. The details of the narrative only add force to the romantic defects we expect in both of them and their growth and development are truly marvelous to watch. This is not a love story. Instead, it is a coming-of-age tale starring two of our favorite characters."
Philip K Jones

Also from MX Publishing

Also from MX Publishing

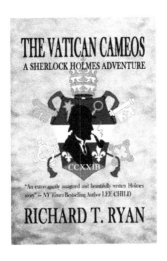

When the papal apartments are burgled in 1901, Sherlock Holmes is summoned to Rome by Pope Leo XII. After learning from the pontiff that several priceless cameos that could prove compromising to the church, and perhaps determine the future of the newly unified Italy, have been stolen, Holmes is asked to recover them. In a parallel story, Michelangelo, the toast of Rome in 1501 after the unveiling of his Pieta, is commissioned by Pope Alexander VI, the last of the Borgia pontiffs, with creating the cameos that will bedevil Holmes and the papacy four centuries later. For fans of Conan Doyle's immortal detective, the game is always afoot. However, the great detective has never encountered an adversary quite like the one with whom he crosses swords in "The Vatican Cameos.."

"An extravagantly imagined and beautifully written Holmes story" (Lee Child, NY Times Bestselling author, Jack Reacher series)

Lightning Source UK Ltd.
Milton Keynes UK
UKOW01f0025120917
309021UK00010B/651/P